CHRISTMAS PAJAMAS

Written by: Stephen Gardner

Illustrated by: Andrea Taylor

This book is fully dedicated to The Most High God.
Thank you for putting this story into my mind.
Thank you for helping me find the artist.
Thank you for allowing me to share it.

Thank you to my wife, Kacey and my children, Gavin, Halle and Julia for supporting me. Thank you also to Andrea, the illustrator, for helping bring my story to life with your beautiful artwork.

"For God So Loved The World,
That He Gave His Only Begotten Son,
That Whosoever Believeth In Him
Should Not Perish, But
Have Everlasting Life."
-John 3: 16

The funeral for James' mother had just ended. The family was grateful to have been able to spend one last Thanksgiving with her before she passed. She was a loving mother and an incredible grandmother. As James and his wife, Sarah, walked back to their car, their five year-old son Joshua asked, "What happens after we die? And where is Grandma now?"

These were deep questions to be asked by someone so young. Joshua always had a knack for deep and thought-provoking questions.

Not fully knowing how to describe life after death or even heaven, Sarah responded, "We go to heaven to be with God and Jesus. Grandma is now in heaven."

After several minutes of silence Joshua interrupted the quiet car ride home by asking, "What is heaven like? Can I go there someday?"

Looking at each other, James gave Sarah a look that seemed to say, *You go ahead and answer this one; I'm driving.* But in all honesty, James did not know how to describe heaven, but felt that whatever it was, he knew his mother would be there. James was familiar with the concept of heaven. His mother had taken him to church from the time he was a newborn, but he had no clue how to describe it, especially not to a five year old.

Up until this moment, Sarah had not given heaven a whole lot of thought either. After all, her parents were still alive and so were all of her siblings. "Heaven is a wonderful place," she replied. "It's like a big family reunion where we get to see our family and spend time with God. Think of it as the best place you can imagine, only better. Grandma is there now and so are the rest of our family members that have already died."

Sarah didn't know if Joshua would understand, but he seemed to be content with her answer and did not press her with 20 questions like he normally did. They spent the rest of the car ride home in silence, but Sarah could see that the wheels in little Joshua's head were turning.

Christmas arrived quickly and the family had a wonderful time. It was their favorite holiday. Each Christmas they would buy new pajamas, watch all their favorite movies and eat all of their favorite treats. Every night Joshua would ask his parents, "How many more sleeps until Christmas?" They went caroling as a family, sledding, read the story of Jesus' birth and spent lots of time together. What none of them knew then was that this would be Joshua's last Christmas. Had they known, they would have soaked up every last second they could with their precious son.

That next spring they lost Joshua in a school bus accident. It was nobody's fault, but the event was tragic, causing unspeakable heartache for both James and Sarah.

As the years passed, the couple did their best to put on a happy face, but the pain of losing their son hovered in their minds constantly. The couple had always believed in God, and in heaven and in Jesus, but now it was hard to believe in something that once brought them peace.

They struggled to understand God's plan because the pain of losing Joshua had cast such a heavy shadow over their fragile faith. Why was he gone? Where was he now? How could this have happened to us? These questions and many more washed over them daily like a violent storm.

For three years the couple prayed for answers, searched their scriptures, attended support groups and tried to find relief from the pain. For three years they felt small impressions, found small amounts of comfort and endured the best they could. However, the lack of understanding and solid reassurance left them feeling empty. With Christmas just a day away, they just wanted to know that Joshua was OK.

On Christmas Eve they spent time with Sarah's family, singing, swapping presents and trying to enjoy time off from work. The truth was they had grown to hate Christmas. It was lonely and hard. So hard. They stopped most of their Christmas traditions. No new pajamas. No movies. It only brought them pain to think of all the Christmases' they wouldn't have with Joshua. That night the two of them knelt in prayer before going to bed and asked to know that their son was OK. They asked that Christmas could be a special time for them again. They asked that the pain of Joshua's absence be eased. They asked that somehow they could have greater understanding of God's plan for them. As James lay in bed, his heart ached and his nightly anxiety took over. That night, however, James had a dream. A wonderful and tender dream.

In the dream James found himself alone in a dark and cold forest-- cold, not because it was winter, but because it was devoid of light and warmth. To make things worse, he had on nothing but his pajamas. As he shivered, wondering where he was, his eye caught sight of a faint light on a hill in the distance. He headed off in the direction of the light, but the trail was wet and slippery.

Several times he fell, but he felt encouraged to keep pursuing the light ahead. As he exited the woods he saw a great stone mansion on top of a hill. This was the source of the light he had seen and been drawn towards. As he approached the great stone mansion and walked up the path that led to the massive home, he could hear music and laughter. There seemed to be a party going on.

As he neared the side of the home he could see into the interior of the home through a window. There was indeed a large and fancy party being held. Not knowing where he was or who lived in this beautiful mansion, he approached the window with caution. On the inside he could see large tables of food - cakes and sandwiches and fruit of all kinds. He could see a small orchestra playing live music and even recognized Silent Night being played. He could see people were dancing and laughing and enjoying themselves.

All that attended the party were dressed in their very best. The men were in tuxedos and the women were in gowns. Even the children were dressed beautifully for the occasion. It seemed to James that this was a very special place and that an extraordinary event was being celebrated. He did not want to interrupt the party, but he also didn't know where he was or why he was there. He needed help.

Just then his eyes filled with tears, his throat tightened and his heart swelled with emotion. On the inside of the great stone mansion he could see his son Joshua through the window. Joshua was dressed in the same handsome suit James and Sarah had picked out for his funeral. He was dancing and laughing and enjoying himself. How could this be? How could my son be here, alive and dancing? James began to cry and then to weep; at first because of sadness, but then because of joy and true happiness. His son was alive!

James watched for several minutes more. He could see that his son was dancing with his late mother. How could they be here together? Confused and wanting to be with his son, he began to bang on the window and yell. He wanted nothing more than to erase the distance that stood between him and his precious little boy. If it were possible, he would have broken down the walls to get inside.

Suddenly a man dressed in a tuxedo leaned out a window on the second floor and interrupted James.

"Can I help you, sir?" asked the man.

"My son is inside and I need to see him! I haven't seen him in years," explained James with an emotional shrill in his voice.

He could hardly hold back his emotions as he attempted to speak with the man. He desperately wanted to be inside and hold his son. The man in the window above told James he was welcome to come inside, but that Samuel, the owner of the home, would never allow him to come in with those dirty, torn pajamas. It wouldn't be right to allow someone with such dirty clothing to join the party.

For the first time James noticed the condition of the pajamas he was wearing. The pajamas had stains all over them. Some were as red as crimson and others as dirty as engine oil. The pajamas also had rips and tears that could not be repaired. Just as James was about to lose hope, the man suggested he walk to the front of the house and speak with the homeowner's son. As the man slipped his head back inside the house, James thought to himself that no one was going to let a stranger in dirty pajamas into a fancy, private party.

James looked inside the party for a second time. For a moment he felt panicked but the feeling soon melted once he could see his son Joshua and his mother dancing and laughing again. He again noticed that not a single person inside was dressed in anything but their very best. Perhaps there was another way inside!

Although the inside of the great stone mansion was well-lit and bright, the outside afforded him shadows and darkness to sneak about. At first James tried sneaking around to the back of the house, but the back door was locked. He tried lifting each of the windows around back but those too were locked and appeared very solid and very heavy. Although out of character, James even tried breaking a window but he could not break the glass. He grimaced that he had even tried such a thing.

As James came back around to where he was before, the man from the second story window again poked his head out and said, "Perhaps the homeowner's son could help you. He is the one that helped me get inside when I first arrived," recommended the man.

Wanting nothing more than to be allowed inside and to see his son again, James walked around to the front of the house. The front entrance was ornate and beautiful. As he neared the entrance, James noticed twelve large stone pillars that held up a large pavilion that was brightly lit. Since the moment he saw his son, all James could think about was how to get inside.

As James approached the house and crossed from the dark of night into the light of the pavilion, he did his best to collect his thoughts and emotions before voicing out loud, "I am looking for the homeowner's son." Just then a man walked out and said he was the homeowner's son.

"My name is Jon, how can I help you?" said the man.

James explained the best he could about how he had arrived at the home and that his son and his mother were inside. He also asked if there were any possible way he could be allowed inside to see them. Even if just for a minute.

The homeowner's son looked at James with compassion but also observed his pajamas. "Unfortunately, you cannot be allowed inside wearing those pajamas. This is a special event by invitation only and has certain dress standards for admission. My father is very strict about who is allowed inside," Jon explained.

As James looked down at his pajamas he saw again just how dirty and worn they appeared. Suddenly, he became embarrassed and the pajamas felt like heavy chains resting on his body. Unexpectedly, he felt very uncomfortable and restricted. He was sorry for his appearance and what it must have taken to get them so dirty and so worn. There he stood in the light, no longer able to hide his pajamas. He felt helpless as there was no way for him to wash or mend them.
James murmured softly, "This is all I have."

Just then James' hope slipped away and he felt shame and despair replace his hope for seeing his family again. With a heavy head and an even heavier heart, James turned away and began to walk back towards the dark and cold forest from where he came. If he couldn't see his son again, perhaps he could at least hide his shame. All of a sudden, he felt a firm grip on his shoulder and heard Jon ask him to please not go just yet.

"My father is a strict man, but he is also kind and trusts my judgment. Perhaps he will let you in on my word and my invitation," Jon said with a compassionate and forgiving voice.

Jon pulled James aside and spoke to him quietly for nearly an hour. Their conversation was private and emotional. As Jon spoke, he pointed to different parts of James' pajamas. Each stain and each tear seemed to have a history; some of them good and many of them not. As he realized what the stains and rips represented, it pained James to speak out loud about most of them. However, it appeared as if Jon felt even sorrier than James as he patiently listened.

One particular tear caught Jon's attention. It was the pajama shirt pocket over James' heart.

"What is this tear from?" Jon inquired.

"That tear is from the pain my wife and I felt as we lost our son Joshua. It's not a tear we have known how to mend or repair. Each year it seems to worsen. I miss him so much sometimes I can't even breathe," James said. "I don't know how to heal the pain."

Together the two men stood in silence, both of them with tears running down their faces; both appearing to relive the pain of that loss.

"I am so sorry you lost your son," Jon said. "I can see that your pain is deep. I can also see that your doubt was dark and that despair has been an unwelcome friend. I am sorry you and your wife have had to carry this pain."

"It's not fair," James cried. "It's not fair to lose your child. It's not fair to see my wife suffer. Life can be so hard and at times even cruel. I cannot understand it."

"Complete fairness and equity cannot be had in your world, but you must trust that all can and will be made right in the end," shared Jon. "Temporary sorrows will one day be made into eternal joys."
Jon's face looked as if he possessed a great empathy for pain and loss. Perhaps he too had suffered great hardship. His caring was earnest and real.

"Have we met before?" James questioned as he wiped away his tears. "It feels as if we know each other well."

"We met a long time ago," shared Jon. "But it was so long ago that you probably can't remember, but I do. I know you very well."

Then Jon continued, "I will lend you something of mine. You can use my name and my invitation to gain entrance to the party. It is the only way they will let you in, but you must change."

Jon slowly shuffled into the house as if he were weary from their emotional conversation. He was away for what seemed like an eternity. He then returned with one of his own tuxedos for James to borrow. The two stepped to a quiet and private area to the side of the door where Jon laid the clothing on what looked like a tall stone bench. Jon then helped James change out of his dirty pajamas into his tuxedo.

The heaviness of the pajamas was gone. The embarrassment of the dirty clothes was replaced with a feeling of confidence. The tuxedo felt as if it were tailored just for James. As James looked up at Jon he could visibly notice how much taller and larger Jon was than himself. Yet, the suit seemed to fit just exactly right. He felt like a new man in Jon's clothes.

As the two finished dressing James, it was obvious that something had changed in Jon's countenance. He looked pre-occupied. Troubled even. Like he was working something out in his mind. James hoped he had not said or done something to affect Jon's mood.

With a softer than normal voice Jon said, "Enjoy the party and we shall see you again another day."

As James started towards the door, Jon placed a white stone in his hand and told him it would allow him to go inside the great stone mansion. On the back side of the stone, James ran his finger over the letters J.O.N.

As he looked back at Jon, he felt mixed feelings of gratitude and sorrow. He felt he owed Jon a great debt, but had no way of repaying him for his kindness. Had it not been for Jon, James would not have been allowed inside.

As he reached for the door knob of the large wooden door, James noticed the intricate detail on the door knob. It was a lamb and a lion standing on their hind legs in the act of playing together. It was both strange and beautiful. James then twisted the knob and opened the door, knowing that his son was just on the other side.

As the door opened, the brightness of the house left him nearly blind. It took several minutes for his eyes to adjust to the light. As his vision returned to him, the first person he saw standing in front of him was his son Joshua. He ran to him and embraced him. He told him how much he loved him and missed him. How much his mom loved him and missed him, too. He cried great tears of joy to see his mother and hold his son once more.

For the next few hours they danced and laughed and enjoyed themselves. Joshua told his father how one day he found himself alone on a well-lit path that led to this very home. How a man named Jon met him and helped him find his grandma. To hear his son's laugh once more and know that he had been cared for filled James' heart with love and gratitude.

As the night rolled on, Joshua introduced his father to the homeowner, Samuel. James felt a very familiar feeling as he shook Samuel's hand, like they had known each other for a thousand years. Samuel had the most familiar face James had ever seen. He seemed to know this face better than he knew his own.

"Have we met before?" James asked. "Because I feel like I know you. I felt like I knew your son, too."

Samuel spoke in a very gentle, but authoritative voice.

"Yes, I know you, James. I know your son and I also know your wife, Sarah. I have always known you and been mindful of you. You cannot understand everything now, but trust me and know that one day you will understand it all. In the meantime, please enjoy the party I have arranged for you and your son to be with me and my son."

James could sense that it pleased Samuel very much to be able to provide him this experience.

As the party wound down, James could feel it was time to go. He did not want to leave, but knew he must. He walked Joshua to his bedroom in the great stone mansion and helped him change into his Christmas pajamas. He tucked him into bed one last time.

His son then asked him, "How many more sleeps until we can see each other again?" James did not know, but knew that they would see each other again. He kissed his son goodbye and told him how much he loved him. James again thanked his mother for watching over his son and told her how much he loved her, too.

Joshua then said, "Tell Mom I love her and that she was right. Tell her that heaven is like the best place she can imagine, but better."

As James was leaving the house, he ran into the man from the upper window. He thanked him for sharing the idea to find the homeowner's son. The man said it was no problem and that everyone in the house was there because of the son. James didn't fully understand what the man meant, but again thanked him for his kind instructions.

As James left the party he looked for Jon so as to thank him one last time and return the borrowed tuxedo. This night was a gift; a kindness he would never be able to repay. Jon could not be found, but near the stone changing bench there was a handwritten note and a clean pair of pajamas. James changed into the fresh pajamas. *Are these my pajamas?* he wondered. Reaching around to look at the tag, he could see that his name was on the pajamas. There were no more stains and no more tears. The pajamas were spotless and without flaw. How could this be?

James carefully unfolded the letter and read:

"The pajamas are not a sum total of all the good and bad one has done in his life. Rather, they are a canvas of expression, showing the person we are becoming. Keep your pajamas unspotted and know that any tears can be mended and any stains can be cleaned. All will be made right one day. Fear not, only be believing." -J.O.N.

James then walked back towards the dark forest. The farther he went, the less light he had to guide him. As he strolled down the path he could hear the music and laughter start up again as if the party were just beginning.

Just before leaving the mansion's grounds, James noticed Jon exiting the dark woods towards the great stone mansion. He held a tiny, little baby girl dressed in bright, white pajamas in his arms. She seemed happy and pure and unafraid. Jon also looked happy. No words were exchanged, only a smile shared between them and a warm feeling. It gave James great comfort to know his son was met by someone so kind when Joshua had arrived.

Suddenly James was back in his house, back in his own bed and back in his usual pajamas. It took him a second to understand where he was. He then climbed out of bed, knelt next to it and humbly offered a prayer of gratitude to the Lord for this special dream. He then woke his wife and told her the details of the dream. Together they cried and held each other as they thought about how there were far better things ahead of them. This Christmas dream gave them hope and healing as they waited for the time when they would see and hold their son again.

That morning, Sarah felt light and brightness enter her life again. The grief was not gone, but the burden felt lighter. With renewed hope for the future, she went online and ordered two new pairs of Christmas pajamas.

The End

NOTE FROM THE AUTHOR

In my life, I have described returning to heaven like showing up at a fancy party in dirty pajamas. I won't have to wait for God's judgement. I'll be able to see that my dress and cleanliness aren't up to heaven's standards and I will dismiss myself from the party. The contrast of my condition with the conditions of heaven will be glaringly obvious.

As I've gained understanding of God's plan and the role of Jesus Christ, I've come to believe that the Savior will not be asking me to leave, but rather will be asking me to stay. I believe I will have a tender reunion with Jesus where I will have to admit how utterly dependent I am upon His good name and His good graces.

No amount of good deeds will allow us into the party. It will only be because of Jesus Christ that we will enter heaven. It is His name and His infinite and eternal Atonement that will cover us and wrap us in the proper heavenly attire.

I am not ashamed of my testimony of Jesus Christ. I am grateful to my Savior for his willingness to take my place, to cover my sins and to patiently help me learn heaven as there is no way I can earn heaven. He has taken our place as the Lamb of God and his sacrifice is enough.

This story came into my mind as a sudden flash. I saw and felt most of it in an instant. I cannot explain it, but I trusted the story was meant to be told so I went to my office and wrote the story you have read today. I hope it will give you an idea of what heaven could be like and how your personal interaction with Jesus Christ and our Father in Heaven might go.

Christmas Pajamas

Stephen E. Gardner

Your ISBN: **9781692585181**

To see more artwork from the illustrator, Andrea Taylor, visit her Instagram page at **@onecreativelife** .

This book is dedicated to Thor Thompson, Tanner Ault, Maely Anderson and anyone else who has lost a child. May God comfort us all until we can be with you again.

Made in the USA
Coppell, TX
10 December 2022